# Over in the Arctic

## Where the Cold Winds Blow

By Marianne Berkes

Illustrated by Jill Dubin

Dawn Publications

Over in the Arctic
Where the cold waters run,
Lived a mother polar bear
And her little cub one.

"Roll," said the mother.
"I roll," said the one.
So they rolled on the ice
Where the cold waters run.

Over in the Arctic
Hopping like a kangaroo,
Lived a mother Arctic hare
And her leverets two.

"Thump," said the mother.
"We thump," said the two.
So they thumped on the tundra
Hopping like a kangaroo.

2

Over in the Arctic
Paddling in the icy sea,
Lived an old mother walrus
And her little calves three.

"Kick," said the mother.
"We kick," said the three.
So they kicked with their flippers
Paddling in the icy sea.

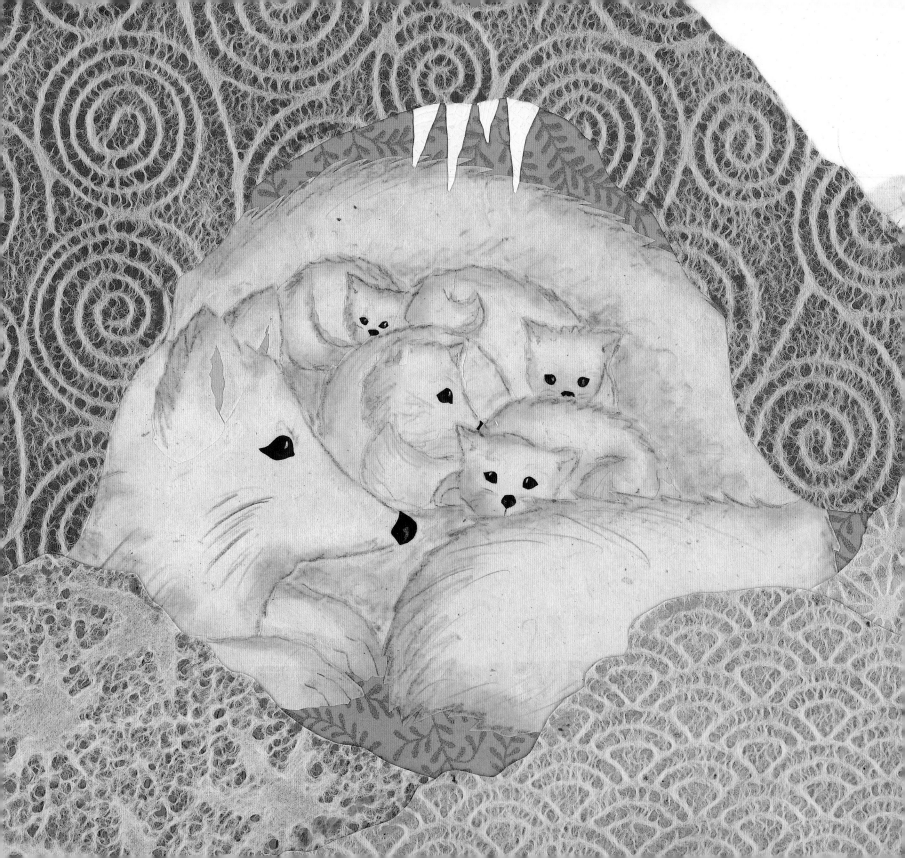

Over in the Arctic
Curled up on a frosty floor,
Lived a mother Arctic fox
And her little kits four.

"Hide," said the mother.
"We hide," said the four.
So they hid and they waited
Curled up on a frosty floor.

Over in the Arctic
Where they dip and they dive,
Lived a white mother whale
And her little calves five.

"Click," said the mother.
"We click," said the five.
So they clicked and they whistled
Where they dip and they dive.

Over in the Arctic
Where the cold waters mix,
Lived a furry mother seal
And her little pups six.

"Breathe," said the mother.
"We breathe," said the six.
So they came up for air
Where the cold waters mix.

6

Over in the Arctic
Gliding up toward heaven,
Lived a mother snowy owl
And her little owlets seven.

"Swoop," said the mother.
"We swoop," said the seven.
So they swooped as they flew,
Gliding up toward heaven.

7

Over in the Arctic
Where some creatures migrate,
Lived a mother snow goose
And her little goslings eight.

"Honk," said the mother.
"We honk," said the eight.
So they honked and flew south
Where some creatures migrate.

8

Over in the Arctic
Where the sun didn't shine,
Lived a mother wolverine
And her little kits nine.

"Growl," said the mother.
"We growl," said the nine.
So they growled and they grumbled
Where the sun didn't shine.

9

Over in the Arctic
In a deep dark den,
Lived an old father wolf
And his little pups ten.

"Howl," said the father.
"We howl," said the ten.
So they howled in a pack
From their deep dark den.

10

Over in the Arctic
Where the cold winds blow,
Arctic animals are living
In the water and the snow.

"Name us," say the animals,
"From ten to one."
Then go back and start over
'Cause this rhyme isn't done.

Over in the Arctic
You can "spy" with your eyes
To find more Arctic creatures—
Every page has a surprise!

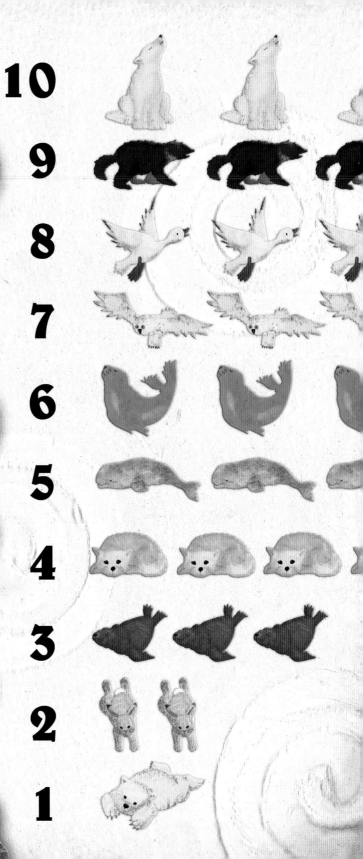

Find the hidden animals

Ermine

Lynx

Narwhal

Ptarmigan

Arctic Tern

Dall Sheep

Musk Ox

Caribou

Ground Squirrel

Lemming

# Fact or Fiction?

In this variation of "Over in the Meadow," all the Arctic animals behave as they have been portrayed. Polar bears do *roll*, snowy owls *swoop*, and Arctic wolves *howl*. That's a fact! But do they have the number of babies as in this rhyme? No, that is fiction. While mother polar bears usually have one or two cubs, the Arctic wolf usually has four or five babies, and the Arctic fox can have as many as 14 babies at one time.

Nature has very different ways of ensuring the survival of different species. The mother wolf nurses her pups, but when the pups are able to eat meat, the whole wolf pack helps feed the pups. A whole herd of walruses will come together to protect their babies from polar bears and killer whales. Both mother and father snowy owl watch over their owlets together. But a mother wolverine tends to her young entirely by herself.

# The Arctic Tundra

The Arctic Tundra is a treeless plain. During the long dark winter it is covered with ice and snow. All year long the ground is frozen—this is called *permafrost*—and plants cannot sink roots into frozen ground. But in summer, when the sun shines 24 hours a day, the snow and the top layer of soil thaw, creating huge soggy marshes and lakes. Dwarf plants can then grow. Melting ice and snow create many puddles where vast numbers of insect eggs hatch, which in turn attracts huge numbers of birds that come from faraway places to nest and raise their young. Whales also migrate as the icy Arctic Ocean warms up and swarms with sea life. But by October when the sun sets and doesn't rise again until February, winter returns and Arctic creatures must adapt to the harsh environment.

How do Arctic animals *adapt* to these extreme conditions? They have heavy fur and a thick layer of fat called *blubber* which protects them. Many Arctic land animals even have fur on the bottoms of their feet to help them walk in snow. Whales have blubber under their skin which keeps them warm even in icy water. Some Arctic animals have a coat that blends in with the color of their surroundings. This *camouflage* hides them from prey they are trying to catch, or from predators trying to catch them. Some animals *hibernate*, or go into a deep sleep, during the cold winter. Other animals go south, or *migrate*, to find warmer winter weather.

# The "Hidden" Arctic Animals

 **ERMINE.** This type of weasel is a ferocious hunter with a keen sense of smell. Ermines have long bodies, which turn white in winter. Because they are slender they can fit down into other burrowing animals' tunnels and hunt them down.

**A LYNX** is a fierce cat that is related to a bobcat. It lives in Arctic forests near the tundra but not on the tundra itself. They have unusually large paws that act as snow shoes. Lynxes stalk their prey and can leap up to 10 feet. Their powerful jaws and sharp teeth can kill prey with one bite.

**NARWHALS** are toothed whales that live in the frigid Arctic Ocean. The male has a very long, twisted tusk so it is sometimes called a "unicorn whale." Narwhals have bluish-gray skin with white blotches and can grow to about 16 feet long.

**PTARMIGANS** are chicken-like birds with feathered feet to help them walk in snow. They can fly, but spend most of the time on the ground. The ptarmigan is the state bird of Alaska. It does not migrate but stays in the Arctic all year round.

**ARCTIC TERNS** are champion long-distance travelers! When they migrate, they fly over 20,000 miles each year from the Arctic to Antarctic and back. The tern swoops down into the water to catch fish.

**MUSK OXEN** are large, horned animals with shaggy, long fur that hangs to the ground. They huddle together in herds and protect their young from predators by closing ranks. They are well-adapted to the cold Arctic environment.

**CARIBOU** are members of the deer family. They wander in large herds across the tundra. Related to reindeer, both males and females have antlers, but the males, or *bulls*, are larger. Males lose their antlers in the winter. In winter they shove snow out of the way with their shovel-like hooves to find food, mostly lichen, underneath.

**DALL SHEEP** have curved horns and are closely related to goats. They have a furry coat that protects them from the cold. A rough pad on the bottom of their hooves helps them move well on uneven ground.

**ARCTIC GROUND SQUIRRELS** are plump rodents that live in colonies and hibernate during the winter. They eat constantly in spring and summer, and store food in their burrows so that when they wake up from their seven-month sleep they will have something to eat.

**LEMMINGS** are small rodents that looks like furry hamsters. They build tunnels with many rooms in which they live during the winter. In the spring they eat roots and berries, and gather seeds for winter. Lemmings are eaten by many animals, including the snowy owl and Arctic fox.

# About the Arctic Animals

**POLAR BEARS** have heavy, water-repellent fur with a thick layer of blubber underneath so they can swim in freezing water. They are often found on top of floating chunks of ice called *ice floes* and **roll** their bodies to cool down if they get too warm. Fur between their toes keeps them from slipping on ice and snow. At the onset of winter, the female digs an underground snow den where she gives birth to one or two **cubs**, and nurses them through the winter. In the spring she teaches them to hunt for seals.

**ARCTIC HARES** *thump* over the snow, racing from predators with powerful hind legs. In winter many hares huddle together to stay warm in a shelter they dig in the snow. Their brilliant white coat is an excellent camouflage. They dig through the snow to find and eat willow bark and mosses. In summer they eat buds, berries, and leaves. Females give birth to two to eight babies. Soon the **leverets** look like their parents and can breed the following year.

**WALRUSES** have large ivory tusks, which can sometimes be three feet long, and can be hooked into ice to pull their enormous bodies out of the water and onto ice. Walruses often weigh between 2,000 and 3,000 pounds. Walruses like to be together, and when not in the water, they huddle together to protect their babies from predators. When a walrus swims, it **kicks** its big back flippers and wriggles its whole body to push through the water. In the water, the **calf** often rides on its mother's back, holding on with front flippers. They dine on clams, worms, snails, and various animals found on the ocean floor.

**ARCTIC FOXES** turn white in winter to match the snow. They curl their bushy tails around themselves like a blanket. Their tiny ears minimize heat loss. Fur on the bottom of their feet keeps frost out. Foxes eat meat, plants and insects, often digging for food with sharp teeth and curved claws. When food is scarce, they *hide* near polar bears, waiting to eat the scraps the bears may leave behind. Females give birth to a large number of **kits**, up to 14 in a litter.

**BELUGA WHALES** are sometimes called "sea canaries" because they often "sing" loudly with *clicks*, clacks, squeaks, whistles and bell-like sounds. The "music" can last for hours. The sounds bounce off various objects and, like bats, they hear the echoes. This ability is called *echolocation*. The echoes enable them to know where things are under water, including prey, without having to see them. Belugas are mammals and need to breathe. Echolocation helps them find small breathing holes when most of the sea is covered by ice. Beluga whales grow to about 15 feet long and often migrate in large groups called pods. Females give birth to a single gray **calf**, which turns white as it matures.

**SEALS** are related to walruses and sea lions. They have a layer of blubber beneath their skin which helps keep heat from leaving their bodies. Blubber serves as food storage also. Several different kinds of seals live in the Arctic, spending most of their lives in the icy water. As mammals, they must **breathe**; and because they swim underwater for up to eight minutes, they have to make good use of air. When under water, their heart rate slows down and they use their oxygen very efficiently. The mother seal gives birth on land or on floating ice to just one **pup** and nurses it until it is ready to swim.

**SNOWY OWLS** glide over the tundra, scanning the landscape with keen eyesight. Suddenly they *swoop* down and catch prey while still in flight. Unlike many owls, the snowy owl has to hunt during the near-constant brightness in summer as well as the near-constant darkness of the long winter. Because there are no trees, their nests are on the ground. The female lays four to fifteen eggs. Both parents bring food to the owlets, who learn to fly at about nine weeks. The young owls, especially males, get whiter as they get older.

**SNOW GEESE** migrate to the tundra to breed. They mate for life and produce two to six creamy white eggs in a shallow ground nest. The family remains together the first year, even though the goslings can swim and eat on their own within 24 hours after they hatch. When winter comes, the family joins a huge *honking* flock heading south. Snow geese are strong flyers. They often fly in a V-shaped formation; the goose in front reduces the wind resistance for those following. Flying in formation also reduces the risk of collision.

**WOLVERINES** are very strong, very aggressive, and have a deep *growl*. They look like small brown bears with cream colored markings, but are actually the largest member of the weasel family. Wolverines eat birds, eggs, fish, plants, roots and fruit, as well as mammals. They have a special gland that produces a strong musk smell. If they kill more food than they can eat, they spray the remainder with their musk and store it underground. No other animal will be interested in the smelly food. In winter the female gives birth to three or four **kits** which she tends by herself in a den dug into the snow.

**ARCTIC WOLVES** have good eyesight and hearing, and a keen sense of smell. They tolerate sub-zero temperatures, up to five months of darkness, and weeks without food. Their distinctive *howl* may signal the beginning and ending of a hunt, or be a warning to other wolf packs. The female gives birth in a den, usually to four or five pups. The male brings them food at first; later the whole pack shares the job, feeding them with regurgitated meat from a kill.

# Tips from the Author

*Over in the Arctic* offers some wonderful opportunities for extended activities. Here are a few suggestions:

- Ten different verbs were used in the story to show how each animal behaves. Act them out as you read or sing the story.

- Ask: What were the ten parents called as babies?

- Discuss: Which creatures in this book migrate? Which ones stay in the Arctic all year?

- Compare ears, noses, tails and toes of Arctic animals to some animals living in warm habitats.

- To find out how blubber keeps an animal warm, fill a zip-lock sandwich bag $\frac{1}{2}$ full with Crisco shortening. Flatten it down and then place it into another zip-lock bag. Place your hand palm down into the second bag so that the layer of the Crisco-filled bag covers your palm. Place your covered hand in a bowl of ice water. Now put your bare hand in the bowl. Feel the difference?

## Let it snow!

- On a winter walk, identify animal tracks.

- Fill spray bottles with water and drops of food coloring. Paint on the snow.

- Freeze some black construction paper so you have it ready for the next snow fall. Go outside and let some snowflakes fall on the frozen paper. Examine them with a magnifying glass.

- Where it doesn't snow, make pretend snow pictures by mixing an equal amount of white glue and foam shaving cream in a plastic bowl. Use a small paintbrush or a Q-tip and make an Arctic snow picture on dark blue construction paper. When the picture has dried, the shaving cream will be puffy, just like real snow!

## Arctic bookmarks

Visit the "Educator Tools" link at www.dawnpub.com to get reproducible bookmarks of four Arctic animals in this book that you can share with your readers.

## Discover more about Arctic life!

*Animal Survivors of the Arctic* by Barbara A. Somervill (2004)

*Arctic* by Wayne Lynch (2007)

*Arctic Lights, Arctic Nights* by Debbie Miller (2007)

*At the Poles, Animal Trackers Around the World* by Tessa Paul (1998)

*Guide to Marine Mammals of Alaska* by Kate Wynne and Pieter Folkens (3rd ed., 2007)

*Life Cycle of a Polar Bear* by Rebecca Sjonger and Bobbie Kalman (2005)

*The Polar Bear Family Book* by Thor Larsen and Sybille Kalas (1996)

www.defenders.org/index.php

www.ipy.org

www.mnh.si.edu/arctic

www.pinnipeds.org

www.polarbearsalive.org

I would love to hear from teachers and parents with creative ways to use this book. My website is: www.marianneberkes.com.

# Tips from the Illustrator

The illustrations for this book were created using layers of cut paper. In my studio I have a rainbow of decorative paper to choose from. There are solid colored papers and papers with textures that range from deep embossed lines to delicate swirls. There are papers with all sorts of patterns like Japanese florals, bold dots and intricate prints.

After researching the animals and their habitats, I make a detailed drawing of each illustration. Using a copy of my drawing as a pattern, I cut each piece out of decorative paper. Sometimes I use a toothpick to glue down small pieces. Then I spread a very thin layer of glue to assemble the elements. I then put the whole thing between two sheets of acetate and press it together under the heaviest books I have. This assures that each finished piece will lie flat. It's like putting a puzzle together! Each animal is made up of a variety of glued-together shapes. All the animals are glued to the background. I finish with colored pencils and pastels to add details, shading and emphasis.

You can see a photo of the walrus art on my desk, along with a copy of my drawing that I used for a pattern. You can make a collage of your own. Although most of the paper I use comes from art supply stores, you can find interesting paper all around: in magazines, wrapping paper, or origami paper. Even the lines on notebook paper can be cut and rearranged to make interesting patterns. Look around for inspiration and use your imagination!

Making snowflakes is a fun and simple thing to do! Start with a square paper. Fold it in half diagonally. Fold it in half diagonally again. Once more, fold in half diagonally. Then cut out random shapes from the top and both sides. Open it to see your snowflake, tape ribbon to one of its points, and hang it up, perhaps in front of your window. As you make more snowflakes, make the cuts different and you will have lots of different designs. In nature, snowflakes have six points. But it's difficult to make a six-pointed snowflake with folded paper. These are beautiful even though they have four points.

# Over in the Arctic

## Sung to the tune "Over in the Meadow"

Traditional Tune
Words by Marianne Berkes

O-ver in the Arct-ic where the cold wa-ters run, lived a mo-ther po-lar bear and her lit-tle cub___ one.

"Roll," said the mo-ther. "I roll," said the one. So they rolled on the ice where the cold wa-ters run.

2. Over in the Arctic
Hopping like a kangaroo,
Lived a mother Arctic hare
And her leverets two.

"Thump," said the mother.
"We thump," said the two.
So they thumped on the tundra
Hopping like a kangaroo.

3. Over in the Arctic
Paddling in the icy sea,
Lived an old mother walrus
And her little calves three.

"Kick," said the mother.
"We kick," said the three.
So they kicked with their flippers
Paddling in the icy sea.

4. Over in the Arctic
Curled up on a frosty floor,
Lived a mother Arctic fox
And her little kits four.

"Hide," said the mother.
"We hide," said the four.
So they hid and they waited
Curled up on a frosty floor.

5. Over in the Arctic
Where they dip and they dive,
Lived a white mother whale
And her little calves five.

"Click," said the mother.
"We click," said the five.
So they clicked and they whistled
Where they dip and they dive.

6. Over in the Arctic
Where the cold waters mix,
Lived a furry mother seal
And her little pups six.

"Breathe," said the mother.
"We breathe," said the six.
So they came up for air
Where the cold waters mix.

7. Over in the Arctic
Gliding up toward heaven,
Lived a mother snowy owl
And her little owlets seven.

"Swoop," said the mother.
"We swoop," said the seven.
So they swooped as they flew,
Gliding up toward heaven.

8. Over in the Arctic
Where some creatures migrate,
Lived a mother snow goose
And her little goslings eight.

"Honk," said the mother.
"We honk," said the eight.
So they honked and flew south
Where some creatures migrate.

9. Over in the Arctic
Where the sun didn't shine,
Lived a mother wolverine
And her little kits nine.

"Growl," said the mother.
"We growl," said the nine.
So they growled and they grumbled
Where the sun didn't shine.

10. Over in the Arctic
In a deep dark den,
Lived an old father wolf
And his little pups ten.

"Howl," said the father.
"We howl," said the ten.
So they howled in a pack
From their deep dark den.

**MARIANNE BERKES** has spent much of her life as a teacher, children's theater director and children's librarian. Because she knows how much children enjoy "interactive" stories, she is the author of seven entertaining and educational picture books that make a child's learning relevant. Her books are also inspired by her love of nature. Marianne hopes to open kids' eyes to the magic found in our natural world. She recently retired to spend full time writing as well as visiting schools and presenting at conferences. She is an energetic presenter who believes that "hands on" learning is fun. Her website is www.MarianneBerkes.com.

**JILL DUBIN'S** whimsical art has appeared in over 30 children's books. Her cut paper illustrations reflect her interest in combining color, pattern and texture. She grew up in Yonkers, New York, and graduated from Pratt Institute. She lives with her family in Atlanta, Georgia, including two dogs that do very little but with great enthusiasm. Her website is www.JillDubin.com.

## DEDICATIONS

*To the many children who touch my life. May you work together to protect and preserve the wonder of the Arctic. Love—MB*

*To Clark with love—JD*

Special thanks to Mrs. Purdham and the teachers and students at Seminole Elementary School for their help with the photos for the "Tips from the Author" page.

Thanks also to Mike Taras, Wildlife Education Specialist with the Alaska Department of Fish and Game in Fairbanks for his assistance with the manuscript.

Thanks to Kathy Peters for her help with the photos for the "Tips from the Illustrator" page.

Library of Congress Cataloging-in-Publication Data
Berkes, Marianne Collins.
 Over in the Arctic : where the cold winds blow / by Marianne Berkes ; illustrated by Jill Dubin. -- 1st ed.
   p. cm.
 Summary: A counting book in rhyme presents various Arctic animals and their offspring, from a mother polar bear and her "little cub one" to an old father wolf and his "little pups ten." Includes related facts and activities.
 ISBN 978-1-58469-109-9 (hardcover) -- ISBN 978-1-58469-110-5 (pbk.)
 [1. Stories in rhyme. 2. Animals--Arctic regions--Fiction. 3. Animals--Infancy--Fiction. 4. Arctic regions--Fiction. 5. Counting.] I. Dubin, Jill, ill. II. Title.
 PZ8.3.B4557Ov 2008
 [E]--dc22
                                        2008012259

DAWN PUBLICATIONS
12402 Bitney Springs Road
Nevada City, CA 95959
530-274-7775
nature@dawnpub.com

Manufactured by Regent Publishing Services, Hong Kong
Printed May 2011 in Shenzhen, Guangdong, China

10 9 8 7 6 5 4 3 2

First Edition

Computer production by Patty Arnold, *Menagerie Design and Publishing.*

## ALSO BY MARIANNE BERKES

*Over in the Ocean: In a Coral Reef*, illustrated by Jeanette Canyon — With unique and outstanding style, this book portrays the vivid community of creatures that inhabit the ocean's coral reefs. Its many awards include the National Parenting Publications Gold Award.

*Over in the Jungle: A Rainforest Rhyme*, illustrated by Jeanette Canyon — As with "Ocean," this book captures a rain forest teeming with remarkable creatures, and was named an "Outstanding Product" by iParenting Media for 2007.

*Over in Australia: Amazing Animals Down Under*, illustrated by Jill Dubin — Illustrated with cut paper, children encounter Australia's unique and endearing animals.

*Going Around the Sun: Some Planetary Fun*, illustrated by Janeen Mason — Our Earth is part of a fascinating planetary family: eight planets and an odd bunch of solar system "cousins." Here young ones can get a glimpse of the neighborhood, and our place in the universe.

*Going Home: The Mystery of Animal Migration*, illustrated by Jennifer DiRubbio — A beautiful and intriguing introduction to animals that migrate by land, sea, and air, with generous supporting factual information.

*Seashells by the Seashore*, illustrated by Robert Noreika — Kids discover, identify, and count twelve beautiful shells to give Grandma.

## SOME OTHER NATURE AWARENESS BOOKS FROM DAWN PUBLICATIONS

*If You Were My Baby* by Fran Hodgkins, illustrated by Laura Bryant — A unique blend of love song and non-fiction celebrating the care that exists between the parents and offspring of many species.

*Jo MacDonald Saw a Pond* by Mary Quattlebaum — Yes, "Old MacDonald" not only had a farm, but a pond too! His granddaughter, Jo, learns about the ducks, dragonflies, frog, and other creatures and the sounds they make. E – I – E – I – O!

*The Mini-Habitat Series* by Anthony Fredericks — Six books that lead a young naturalist to look more closely at a community of animals under one rock, on one flower, around one cactus, around one log, in one tidepool, and around one cattail.

*The John Denver & Kids Series* — Picture books based on some of John Denver's most delightful lyrics: *Sunshine On My Shoulders*, *Take Me Home, Country Roads*, *Grandma's Feather Bed*, *Ancient Rhymes: A Dolphin Lullaby*, and *For Baby (For Bobbie)*.

Dawn Publications is dedicated to inspiring in children a deeper understanding and appreciation for all life on Earth. You can browse through our titles, download resources for teachers, and order at www.dawnpub.com, or call 800-545-7475.